OLiVia's
Secret
Scribbles

AMAZING
Acrobats

Kane Miller
A DIVISION OF EDC PUBLISHING

With thanks to amazing acrobats Holly and Tessa, and monkey bar stars Lainey, Bianca, Amelia, Emma, Mikayla, Kenzie and Shifa from Rolling Hills PS—M.C.

For Uncle Stuart and Aunty Karen. Thank you for your wonderful love and support.—D.M.

First American Edition 2019
Kane Miller, A Division of EDC Publishing

First published by Scholastic Australia Pty Limited in 2018.
This edition published under license from Scholastic Australia Pty Limited.

Library of Congress Control Number: 2018943927

Printed and bound in the United States of America

3 4 5 6 7 8 9 10

ISBN: 978-1-61067-841-4

OLIVIA'S
BIG BOOK of
PRIVATE
SECRETS

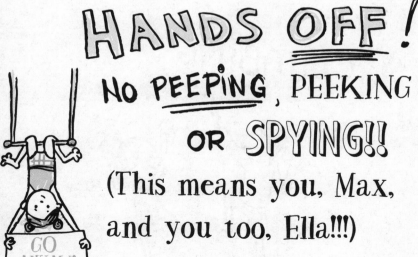

HANDS OFF!
NO PEEPING, PEEKING
OR SPYING!!
(This means you, Max,
and you too, Ella!!!)

Cheeky Monkey Tuesday

The COOLEST THING EVER has been happening at school.

Everyone in my grade has been making up awesome tricks on the playground equipment. Every lunchtime!

We love CLIMBING

and jumping JUMP

and doing FLIPS!

As soon as the bell rang for recess,
Matilda and I grabbed some snacks
from our bags. Then we ran out to the
playground.

Matilda is my new best friend. She moved into the house behind ours a few months ago. We do (almost) everything together. Like playing soccer. And roller-weaving in my driveway. And building stuff in our backyards.

Roller-weaving

BOTH
Feet together

Right leg ONLY

Backward

LEGS CROSSING over

Ava and Daisy were already there, hanging off the monkey bars. And so were Sage and Samira.

"Come and play!" Ava called to us.

So Matilda and I climbed up beside them.

Ava

Daisy

Sage

Samira

ME

Matilda

Then we all swung ourselves
along the rungs, hand by hand.
Just like a bunch of cheeky
monkeys! ☺

That gave me an idea for a new game.
"Let's have a monkey bar
race!" I said, jumping down
again. Everyone else
jumped down too.

"Let's have a monkey bar race!"

"I bet I'll win!" said Samira.

"No, me!" said Sage. "I'm the best! The
fastest and the best!"

Ava went first. She jumped up to the bar and held on tightly. Then she pulled herself along all the rungs, twisting and turning, while we all counted.

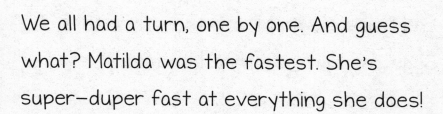

We all had a turn, one by one. And guess what? Matilda was the fastest. She's super-duper fast at everything she does!

🙂livia

Race-to-the-top Wednesday

We played on the playground equipment at school again today. But this time, at recess, we made up amazing NEW tricks on the hammock swing instead.

Here's what we did.

Matilda and I stood in the middle while Ava and Daisy pushed from the sides. Then Sage and Samira jumped on too.

We did all kinds of tricks on the swing.

Jumping. Hopping. Spinning around.

Sage and Samira fell over **six times**.
Matilda and I only fell over twice!

va

Sage

Matilda

ME

Samira

Daisy

Then at lunchtime we did something *even more fun* on the climbing frame.

Matilda called out, "Last one to the top is a rotten egg!" and we raced each other right up to the top of the frame. This time I won!

ME

Matilda

AVa

Sage

Daisy

Samira

Ava dared me to hang upside down from the very top. So I did!

Lots of other kids were looking up at me, pointing and staring.

It felt amazing. Like I was the Queen of the World!

☺livia

After dinner

my PLANS

I've just had a brilliant idea!

Matilda and I are both SUPER AMAZING at doing playground tricks. Especially on the monkey bars. We could put on a show at lunchtime!

Here's my plans for what we could do.

OLIVIA AND MATILDA'S SUPER-AMAZING MONKEY BAR SHOW

IMPORTANT! Race to the monkey bars as soon as the bell goes so we get there first!

Then:

1. Swing along the frame from end to end (forward).

2. Swing back along the frame from end to end (backward).

3. Pull yourself up to the low bar, do a roll around it, then slowly come back down again.

4. Do a backbend while hanging from the double bars.

5. Climb to the top of the climbing frame and sit on the top. Wave to the audience.

6. Hang upside down from the high bar for 20 seconds. Then climb down and take a big bow.

* Remember to bring awesome costumes so we can look like Monkey Bar Superheroes!

** Remember to eat lunch AFTER we've finished all the hanging upside down. ☺

Tiaras

Capes

And guess what? School vacation starts next week. We can practice our show every day on the monkey bars in the park!

It's going to be the best show ever!

☺livia

Mystery Thursday

I told Matilda all about Olivia and Matilda's Super-Amazing Monkey Bar Show on our way to school this morning. She thought it was a brilliant idea too.

"Let's start practicing today!" she said. "Which tricks are we going to do?"

I showed her my plan.

"These tricks
are . . . umm . . .
awesome,"
she said.

But something was wrong. I could tell.

As soon as the bell rang for lunchtime, Matilda and I ran straight over to the monkey bars before anyone else could grab them.

We practiced the tricks for our show.

First forward . . .

FORWARD

and then backward. Over and over again.

BACKWARD

Then we pulled
ourselves up to
the low bar and did
backbends next.

backbends

And each time we did it we got a little bit better.

Ava and Daisy were standing next to the bars, watching. And so were Sage and

Samira. And lots of other kids from our
class.

Lots of other kids started watching us too.
Even the yard-duty teachers came over!

I gave them all
a big wave.

Then I hung upside
down for 20 whole
seconds. It was super
cool!

Everyone clapped and cheered when I
jumped down at the end and did my bow.
Even Mr. Platt and Ms. Weiss!

Then I noticed something.

Matilda wasn't there.

She'd completely vanished!

I looked all over the playground, but I didn't find Matilda until the end of lunchtime. She'd been hiding in the girls' bathroom.

Me: What are you doing in here? I've been looking everywhere for you!
Matilda: Umm . . . I felt a bit sick. So I came in here.

But Matilda didn't look sick. Just sad.

Me: Why did you run away? Everybody loved us!

Matilda: I . . . I couldn't do the last trick.

Me: Why not?

Matilda: I don't like hanging upside down. I'm scared I'll fall.

I'm SCARED.

Me: Oh. Sorry. You should have told me! I could have changed it to something else!

Matilda: I didn't want you to think I was chicken. But now everyone's going to know I am. They'll call me names, just like they did at my last school. ☹

Oh no! Poor Matilda!

Now I feel really bad.

I hope she still wants to be my friend.

☺livia

Fabulous Friday!

The monkey bars were super busy at lunchtime today. Everyone was trying out show tricks just like ours! But Matilda and I played

soccer on the big field with Harry and Nico instead. I could tell that made Matilda *heaps* happier.

She is definitely still my friend! ☺

HARRY

I was a bit sad I didn't get to do more flips and tricks with everyone else though. ☹

But then something *even better* happened when I got home from school!

Nanna Kate came over with an amazing surprise!! She had tickets to the circus for that night and was taking Max, Ella and me!

We all sat together on a long wooden bench inside a big stripy tent. And we had popcorn in paper cups. And drinks with bendy straws!

★ BIG TOP ★
CIRCUS
ADMIT ONE

★ WELCOME ★
TO THE
BIG TOP CIRCUS

Trapeze Artists!
Acrobats!
Clowns!
AND
MUCH MORE!
6pm TONIGHT

BOOK NOW!

My favorite part was when the circus people flew high through the air on swinging bars. Nanna Kate said the people were trapeze artists.

TRAPEZE artists

We saw backflipping acrobats

♥ ELLA Loved these the BEST.
She can do BACKFLIPS too!

and juggling
stilt walkers

This was **Max's** favorite **TRICK.**

and spinning hula-hoopers.

Nanna Kate said she used to do this when she was our age. But I think she might be fibbing.

And then I had another brilliant idea. Matilda and I could put on a bigger, better show in my backyard instead of at school. With juggling! And hula-hooping! And acrobatic tricks! (And no upside-down bits.)

We could be amazing acrobats too!

I'm going to race over to Matilda's place and ask her about it first thing in the morning!

☺livia

PS I really, really, really hope she says yes!

Fingers CROSSED
TOES crossed

Super-Amazing Saturday

Guess what? Matilda *did* say yes! And we spent all day in my backyard, trying out new tricks for our new show!

Our little brothers, Max and Benny and Ollie, came out to watch us.

Benny OLLIE MAX

BOB

THE AUDIENCE

We did forward rolls

FORWARD ROLLS

and backward rolls

Backward

and cartwheels on the lawn.

cartwheeLS

And we took turns spinning hula-hoops around our tummies.

around our tummies

And our ankles.

our ankles

And our necks.

our necks!

I was just tying an old bit of rope to a tree for our next trick when Mom came out to see what we were up to.

MOM

Mom: Olivia! What are you doing?!

Me: Tying this rope to this tree branch, so we can swing from it. Matilda and I are going to be high-flying circus stars!

Mom: Come down! It could break!

Me: Don't worry. I'm using one of my special super-duper knots!

Mom: Olivia! Get down from that tree. Right now!

Me: ☹ ☹ ☹

COME DOWN!

Mom went back inside.

A few minutes later my sister, Ella, came out with a big sign and taped it to the tree.

So Matilda and I decided to do juggling instead.

Juggling looks easy-peasy. Even our teacher, Mr. Platt, can do it. One day, he juggled our fruit from recess. And he didn't drop any of it! So we decided to use fruit too.

MR. Platt

I went back into our house, looking for fruit. There was a big bag of oranges in the pantry. YES! I raced back outside with it.

LOOK what I found!

Perfect!

↑ BAG

I grabbed three oranges out of the UP UP UP! bag. Then I threw the first one UP into the air.

But before I could throw the second one up, the first one came down again.

It landed  SPLAT! on the ground.

Then Matilda had a try. Her orange fell SPLAT! down too.

I shut my eyes
really tight and
made a picture in
my head of the
jugglers in the circus.
It didn't look that
hard when they
did it.

Then I had another try. And another. And
another. And so did Matilda.

But every time, the same thing happened.

SPLAT!

SPLATT!!

SPLATTTT!!

There were squishy bits of orange all
over the lawn.

And all over our feet.

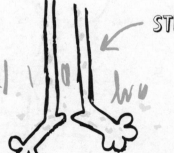

STICKY MESS

And our legs.

Oops!

Mom's going to go bananas
when she finds out!

☺livia

PS She did. ☺

Sensational Sunday

This morning, Matilda and I thought up something new for our show. We're going to be Sensational Stilt Walkers!

We didn't have any real stilts, so Dad helped us to make some out of old bits of wood and strong glue from the shed.

I drew these plans for how to make them.

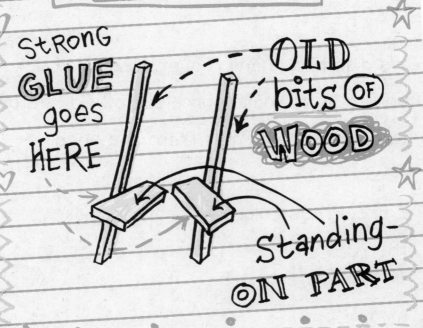

STiLTS
Plans BY oLiVia

STRONG **GLUE** goes **HERE**

OLD bits ⓞⓕ **WOOD**

Standing- **ⓞN PART**

Dad helped me to stick the small pieces of wood to the long pieces with the glue. But our feet kept slipping off the standing-on part!

Next time I use glue, I'll make sure Bob and Donkey stay inside!

BOB

DONKEY

So we cut up some old bandages I found in the linen cupboard into long strips. Then Dad wrapped them tightly around our legs and feet. I felt just like a mummy! ☺

Here's what my new, improved stilts look like!

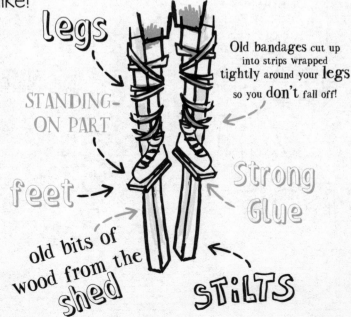

legs

STANDING-ON PART

Old bandages cut up into strips wrapped tightly around your legs so you don't fall off!

feet →

Strong Glue

old bits of wood from the shed

STiLTS

Learning how to walk on our stilts was very tricky. I had to hold on to the outdoor table until I got my balance.

I wobbled from side to side, flapping my arms like a bird.

And then suddenly, I was standing up really straight and tall on my stilts.

I strutted around the backyard. And so did Matilda. Just like the stilt walkers in the circus!

We got better
and better and
faster and faster.
Soon we were
chasing each
other around.

Benny and Ollie and
Max clapped and
cheered.

Matilda: Stilt walking is awesome.
Me: Super awesome.
Matilda: Who needs silly old monkey bar
tricks for our show?

Me: There are so many real circus tricks we can do instead!

Matilda: YES! We're going to be perfect!

And then Bob got in our way and we crashed into each other.

And fell over.

Right into the middle of Mom's veggie garden. Just as Mom came home with pizzas for our lunch.

Oops!

Later that day . . .

Mom banned us from doing any more stilt walking. ☹

So after lunch, we decided to train Bob and Donkey to be circus stars instead!

Matilda and I taught Bob to walk on his hind legs

ME

BOB loves his food.
He'll do anything for
a dog treat!

DOG
Treats

BOB

and beg for his dinner

and do a high five

and push a beach ball along with his nose.

Bob pushing the ball
with his nose!

Donkey was sitting on the
fence watching Bob learn his tricks.

Donkey is our neighbors' cat. He
likes visiting me in my upstairs
bedroom.

He is a big grumpy pants, especially when
you make him do things he doesn't want
to do. Like lying still when you're trying to
pat him.

Or being a detective cat
so you can spy on your
neighbors. ☺

But he loves playing with jingly dangly toys.

And hiding inside laundry baskets. He's always jumping out at people and giving them a fright. Then he drops back down inside again and waits for the next person to come past.

So we invented a trick for him that he can do in our circus show! Here are my plans for it.

All I have to do is dangle the jingly toy over the top of the laundry basket. Donkey will leap up to grab it, then drop back down inside the basket.

And guess what? It worked!

Here's a photo I took of Circus Star Donkey leaping up to catch the jingly dangly toy. ☺

Jingly dangly toy

laundry basket

DoNKey
the leaping CAT!

Donkey and Bob were both amazing! But we still don't have enough tricks yet to put on a show.

☺livia

Marvelous Monday

It's the first day of school vacation today. Yay!

Max and Ella and I went to the library to get new books. Everyone loves reading in our house.

I ran straight to the section that has the books with facts and information.

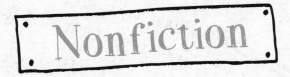

Nonfiction

I wanted to find some new tricks for our show. And look what I found!

But here's the best bit—look what I found taped to the door on the way out!

Have you ever wanted to swing from a trapeze? Ride a unicycle? Or learn how to juggle?

Come to our VACATION CIRCUS SKILLS WORKSHOP

SUNSHINE CENTER
Barkly Street
2pm to 4pm

Every weekday during SCHOOL BREAK

FREE Have fun!

Learn NEW skills!

Make new friends!

I can't believe it!!! There's going to be a circus skills workshop at the Sunshine Center. And it starts this afternoon!

I could learn how to be a real circus star. And learn some new tricks for our show!

I can't wait to tell Matilda. Then all I have to do is get Mom and Dad to say yes. ☺

☺livia

A bit later . . .

Mom and Dad said I can go!

But only if I promise to:

1 Tidy up the stinky mess
I made in my room
doing my "How to make
rotten egg gas" experiment last week.

stinky mess - - - →

2 Make my bed every day.

3 Eat all my vegetables
(especially the green ones).

YUCK!

4 Help Ella load the dishwasher after dinner without complaining.

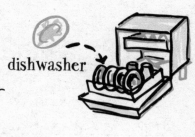

dishwasher

5 Stay out of trouble!

This one might be a bit **HARD!**

YES!

But guess what the best part is? Matilda is coming to the circus workshop too!

After dinner . . .

Circus School was awesome!

And some of my other friends from school were there too!

Ava   Daisy   HARRY   Nico

Our teachers are called Katya and Mitch. They're really bendy, just like the performers we saw at the circus.

Really bendy

Mitch   Katya

And they're funny, just like my teacher, Mr. Platt.

And they're really strong, just like ~~my dad~~ superheroes in comic books and at the movies! ☺

Katya   Mitch

We started off with warm-ups, the same as we do at soccer practice.

First of all we warmed up our legs. We ran across the room, as fast as we could.

Then we hopped like
one-legged kangaroos

and crawled like babies

and walked backward on our
hands and feet with our knees
sticking out, like giant frogs.

Then we warmed up the rest of our bodies.

BeNding OVER BackWard with hands on HiPs

After that, Katya and Mitch dragged huge mats into the middle of the room, so we could do some tumbling.

Yes! I ♡ tumbling.

We did forward rolls and backward rolls.

FORWaRD ROLL   Backward ROLL

Then we learned a cool new move called
double forward rolls.

Matilda lay down on
the mat in front of
me, holding my ankles.
I leaned forward and
grabbed her ankles.

ME

↘

Matilda

Then I did a forward roll
right over the top of her!

ME ↘

Matilda

Now it was Matilda who was
standing up.

Matilda!

→

← ME!

We did heaps of double forward rolls, all the way to the end of the room.

Then Mitch told us to try doing it backward!

We were going really well until I bumped my head and we both got the giggles. And then we fell over in a big heap. And crashed into Ava and Daisy. Who crashed into two sisters called Tessa and Holly.

Oops!

And then they all got the giggles too.

Backward double rolls are really tricky!

I can't wait to find out what we're going
to learn tomorrow!

☺livia

Hula-Hoop Tuesday

Today when we arrived at the Sunshine
Center something was different. There
were long swing things hanging from

the ceiling. They looked just like the swings the flying trapeze artists used at the circus.

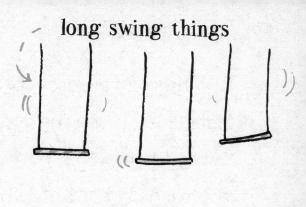

long swing things

Matilda's face went all white, like a fluffy marshmallow.

She tugged my arm. "Do you think we're going to go on those today?"

"I hope so," I said. I couldn't wait!

But then I remembered how scared Matilda is of hanging upside down. And the swing things were much higher up than the monkey bars at school.

So I pretended not to be too excited.

Katya put some jazzy music on and we did our warm-ups again. Then Mitch disappeared behind a curtain and came back with some big boxes. He pulled out lots of different things for us to use.

HULa-HOOPS

and **juggling balls** ~ →

and **fLOWER sticks.** →

Then they showed us all how to use them.

Daisy

Daisy looked just like a hula dancer!

Mimi was a whiz with the flower sticks.

NICO

Nico was the best juggler.

I tried really, really hard to juggle the juggling balls. But I kept dropping them, just like I did with the oranges. They went rolling all over the floor!

I was just about to give up when Mitch came over. He said sometimes you just have to keep trying, even though what you're doing is really, really hard.

So I'm going to practice every day until I can do it, right here in my room. Or out in our backyard. Or on Ella's bed. Hehehe. ☺

The hula-hoops were *easy-peasy*. I spun one around my tummy, and one around my wrist, and one around my ankle.

All at the same time!

But Matilda kept looking up at the swing things. And her hoop kept falling straight down to the ground. ☹

☹livia

Slippery Silk Wednesday

Matilda was sure we'd have to go on the swing things today.

But we didn't. We climbed up and down long strips of silk hanging from the ceiling instead!

Katya showed me how to
wrap the silk around my
ankle to make a foot lock
so I wouldn't fall.

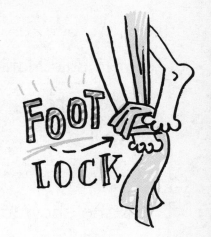

Then we all held on tightly
to the top part of the
silks with both hands, and
moved ourselves up and
down with our feet. It was
awesome!

The circus name
for silk ropes is
tissu.

Katya said Matilda and Ava and I were climbing really well. Like real amazing acrobats!

So she showed us how to do some special tricks. Just the three of us.

Like THiS one

AND THIS one

It was the

BEST Day EVER!

☺livia

Wriggly Worm Thursday

Today was Animal Day at Circus School!

Mitch divided us up into two groups. Matilda and I were together! ☺

We had to use our bodies to make animal shapes, which is really hard. We tried climbing up on each other's shoulders, to make a giraffe with a long neck.

But the higher we went, the trickier it was.

NECK

GiRAFFE

BODY

Our giraffe neck got wobblier and wobblier until **CRASH!** we all came tumbling down.

So we tried to make a crocodile with snapping jaws. But Holly and Tessa kept

getting the
giggles and
our crocodile
collapsed in
the middle.

Holly   Tessa

Then Matilda and Harry had a brilliant idea.
We all joined up together to make a wriggly
worm. And we wiggled and wobbled our
way all around the room!

"Wriggle,

Daisy's group made an elephant. We had to keep out of their way so our worm didn't get squashed!

trunk

ear

tail

ELePHANT

legs

At the end of the session, Katya and Mitch gave us all animal-shaped cookies. Yum!

YUM!

Then Katya told us that two important things are going to happen tomorrow.

1. We're going to learn an exciting new skill.

2. There's going to be a special announcement!

Ava and Daisy and I chatted about what the exciting new skill might be as we were leaving.

Matilda

Daisy

Ava

ME

But Matilda looked like she was going to be sick. ☹

☹livia

Triple-decker Friday

Mitch made the special announcement as soon as we arrived at Circus School today.

We're all going to be performing in a circus show next weekend! And we get to invite our family and friends!

This was FABULOUS news. Now Matilda and I can be in a real circus show, not just in my backyard with squishy oranges!

We each have to choose our three best tricks and practice and practice them for the whole of next week until we sparkle!

YES! It's going to be supercool!

The next thing we did was learn our new exciting special skill.

And guess what it is?

Ta-daaaa!

The long swing things which
are called the trapeze! ☺

Katya showed us how to sit
on the bar and swing

and do backbends
and monkey rolls

and hang upside down.
Without holding on!

Katya

trapeze

ME

BackBends

upside
down

We even tried the triple trapeze!

This time, Matilda didn't hide in the bathroom when it was her turn. She just stood quietly in the corner all by herself, practicing her hula-hooping.

Over and over. And over again.

So as soon as I finished my turn, I ran to the corner and gave her a big hug. And then I had another brilliant idea!

☺livia

Super Surprise Saturday

Matilda came over to my place straight after breakfast, just like we arranged yesterday.

We put our roller skates on and headed out the gate and down the sidewalk.

We skated into the park, past the fountain, and over to the playground.

Then we stopped. Right next to the monkey bars. Only this time, Matilda didn't need to worry about anyone laughing at her, or calling her chicken, like they did at her old school. There was no one else there.

I handed Matilda a sparkly tiara and a shimmering cape from Ella's dress-up box. Ella loves dress up. ☺

Olivia: Put these on.
Matilda: Er, OK . . . why?
Olivia: So you can pretend you're a Monkey Bar Superhero!
Matilda: Oh! Cool!!

Then Matilda climbed up onto the bar, and
tried to hang upside down.

First she just leaned back a teeny, tiny bit.
Then, little by little, she practiced going
all the way. Over and over again. Just like
Mitch told me to do when I kept dropping
all the juggling balls.

First on the low bar.

Then on the medium one.

And finally . . . on the big, tall, high one!

Yes!

She did it!
☺livia

One week later . . .

Spectacular Saturday!

We've been busy, busy, busy all week, practicing our three favorite skills.

And each day we got better. And better.
And better!

And today it was finally . . . SHOWTIME!

Guess what my three
skills were?

Doing climbing tricks on
the silk ropes.

And monkey rolls on the trapeze.

And . . .

juggling!

At the end of the show three of us ran back out again for a special encore on the triple trapeze.

And guess who was hanging upside down from the middle this time?

MATILDA

For our final act, everyone came together
to make one more giant shape.

And the whole audience clapped and
cheered. Especially my mom! ☺

☺livia

Circus Stars Sunday

Now Matilda and I can be amazing acrobats whenever we want!

☺livia

Read them all!

OLiVia'S Secret Scribbles